the

Didi Dodo
FUTURE SPY

series

Book One: Recipe for Disaster
Book Two: Robo-Dodo Rumble
Book Three: Double-O Dodo

the

series

Book One: Inspector Flytrap
Book Two: Inspector Flytrap in The
President's Mane Is Missing
Book Three: Inspector Flytrap in The
Goat Who Chewed Too Much

By TOM ANGLEBERGER

Illustrated by
JARED CHAPMAN

Amulet Books • New York

The Library of Congress has cataloged the hardcover edition as follows:
Names: Angleberger, Tom, author. | Chapman, Jared, illustrator.
Title: Didi Dodo, future spy : in recipe for disaster! / by Tom Angleberger ; illustrated by Jared Chapman.
Other titles: Recipe for disaster!
Description: New York : Amulet Books, 2019. | Summary: When Koko Dodo's secret chocolate sauce is stolen just before an important cooking contest Didi, a dodo bird, devises a daring plan to help--whether he wants her to or not.Identifiers: LCCN 2018018956 (print) | LCCN 2018024277 (ebook) | ISBN 9781683354758 (All e-books) | ISBN 9781419733703 (hardcover pob)
Subjects: | CYAC: Spies--Fiction. | Stealing--Fiction. | Baking--Fiction. | Contests--Fiction. | Dodo--Fiction.
Classification: LCC PZ7.A585 (ebook) | LCC PZ7.A585 Did 2019 (print) | DDC [Fic]--dc23

Paperback ISBN 978-1-4197-3706-0

ABRAMS The Art of Books
195 Broadway, New York, NY 10007
abramsbooks.com

CONTENTS

Opening

nspector Flytrap's phone rang.

And rang.

And rang.

And rang.

Finally, a really loud taped voice said: "Hello, you've reached the office of Inspector Flytrap and Inspector Nina the Goat. They are not in the office today, because Inspector Flytrap's grandmother has come to visit. Please leave a message at the sound of the bleat."

"Bleat," said a very bored taped voice.

"This is Koko Dodo!" I shouted into the phone. "What are you telling me about a grandmother? I've got a BIG DEAL mystery for you to solve! My Super Secret Fudge Sauce has been stolen! Right before the Queen's Royal Cookie Contest! What am I going to do? Who will help me? Who? WHO?"

Then a taped voice said, "Are you still talking? Don't bother. Nina the Goat will probably eat this tape before I get a chance to listen to it anyway. Good-bye."

Click.

I began to sob.

PART 1

Her Majesty's Super Secret Fudge Sauce

Chapter 1

I was still sobbing when someone came into my store, Koko Dodo's Cookie Shop.

She was wearing roller skates. And she came in really, really, really fast. TOO FAST!

She smashed into my cookie case, flew into the air, knocked over a bowl full of chocolate chips, and landed in a fresh batch of snickerdoodle dough.

"Have no fear, Didi Dodo is here!" she said.

"Do you want to buy a cookie?" I asked.

"Well, maybe," she said, "but I really came because I heard you needed help."

"Oh my goodness, I really do! If you can help me, I'll GIVE you the cookie. But . . . how did you know I needed help?"

"I'm Didi Dodo, Future Spy. I know many things and have many daring plans."

"A 'future spy'?" I asked. "Does that mean you're from the future?"

"No."

"Does it mean you can see into the future?"

"No."

"Does it mean you have lots of futuristic gadgets and spy gear?"

"No."

"Then what does it mean?" I asked.

"It means I will be a spy someday."

"Oh," I said.

Then Didi Dodo sprang to her feet—actually, to her wheels—and waved one wing in the air.

She held her beak high.

Her eyes sparkled, and so did the cookie dough stuck to her tail feathers.

"But," she announced, "TODAY IS THAT SOMEDAY!"

Chapter 2

Didi handed me a little card.

It said:

DIDI DODO
FUTURE SPY
(and licensed babysitter)

"Can you also use a spoon?" I asked her.

"Well, sure," she said, "of course I can use a spoon!"

"Great, because I need you to mix up a new batch of snickerdoodle dough! The old batch has too many of your feathers in it!"

I quickly tossed her three eggs, half a stick of butter, two cups of flour, a teaspoon of vanilla, a pinch of salt, four figs (sliced), and three strips of bacon (crispy).

"So," she said while stirring, "I hear your Super Secret Fudge Sauce has been stolen."

"Yes," I said. "It's gone! Oh, boo-hoo! Boo-hoo!"

"Can't you just make some more?" she asked.

"That's the worst part!" I told her, holding up an empty jar. "I am out of the secret ingredient that makes the Super Secret Fudge Sauce so super!"

"Well, what is the secret ingredient?"

"I can't tell you," I told her. "It's a secret!"

"If you want me to help you, you'll have to tell me. Don't worry, I'm a Future Spy, I can keep a secret."

"BUT I CAN'T!" I admitted. "That's why my mom never told me what it was. It's a family recipe!"

"That's weird," said Didi Dodo.

"It's worse than weird!" I shouted. "It's terrible! Because now I can't get more of the secret ingredient to make more of the Super Secret Fudge Sauce to put on the cookies to win the Queen's Royal Cookie Contest, which takes place this afternoon!"

"What's the Queen's Royal Cookie Contest?"

"WHAT'S THE QUEEN'S ROYAL COOKIE CONTEST?" I yelled. "It's the most

important cookie event of the year! Every year, the Queen chooses the best cookie in the world, and every year for the last twenty years that cookie has been MY COOKIE with MY FUDGE SAUCE with MY SECRET INGREDIENT!"

I pointed at my trophies. Didi barely glanced at them!

"And you say this Royal Contest takes place this afternoon?"

"Yes."

"Great! I have a daring plan!"

Chapter 3

A buzzer went off.

I pulled a batch of gingersnaps out of the oven and slid a tray of uncooked gingerbread bigfoots in.

Then I started rolling out some Swedish nut wafer dough.

"Don't you want to hear my daring plan?" asked Didi.

"No," I said. "I do not like daring plans."

"But this daring plan will catch the thief!"

"Do you have any plans that are *not* daring? Maybe an easy, no-problem, foolproof, can't-go-wrong plan? Those are the plans I like!"

"Well, that kind of plan isn't going to catch the thief, get back your fudge sauce, or win you another royal trophy."

"OK," I said. "I'll *listen* to your daring plan."

"Great! So, the first thing we do is—"

BANG BANG SMASH BANG

"WHAT ARE YOU DOING?" she yelled.

"I'm smashing nuts for my Swedish nut wafers!" I yelled back, still smashing.

"Would you please stop that for a minute and listen to my daring plan?"

"Is it OK if I sprinkle the nuts while you explain the plan?" I asked.

"If you must . . ."

"Thank you."

Sprinkle sprinkle sprinkle!

"OK. So here's the plan:

"I have two problems with that plan," I told Didi.

"What? It's a perfect plan!"

"Not quite. First, the cookie contest is at the mall, so there's no throne to leap out from behind."

"Fine, we'll find something else to leap out from behind. What's the other problem?"

"The other problem is that I DO NOT WIN THE TROPHY!" I yelled.

"But you catch the thief!"

"I don't want to catch the thief. I want MY TROPHY!"

"What about justice?"

"Is there a trophy for justice?"

"Hmm . . . not usually."

"Then I don't want justice! I want to win the ROYAL COOKIE CONTEST!"

Didi stopped stirring.

She waved one wing in the air.

She held her head high.

Her eyes sparkled, and so did the butterscotch stuck to her forehead.

"I have a daring plan to do both!"

Interlude

Firist," said Didi Dodo, "we need to go find DJ FunkyFoot."

"Are you kidding with me? I have old-fashioned sugar cookies with rainbow sprinkles in the oven! I can't go looking for a rapper, no matter how funky his feet are!"

"But DJ FunkyFoot isn't a rapper! He's a butler," she said. "AND he's a Chihuahua."

"Gross! What are you telling me about a Chihuahua?"

"A Chihuahua is a kind of dog, and dogs have really powerful noses."

"I don't have time for his powerful nose or his funky feet OR anything else but these cookies!"

"If you want to win that contest, you'd better turn the oven off and put your skates on!"

I turned the oven off. I put my skates on.

"Uh, those are ice skates," said Didi.

"What are you telling me for? I know they are ice skates. I am a former champion ice dancer. Haven't you heard of the Triple Koko? I invented that move!"

"Great, but there's no ice outside. It's the middle of summer. You need roller skates."

"I don't have roller skates."

"Then hop on my back and let's go start my daring plan!"

I hopped on her back. She skated out the door and into the street!

At first, I was worried that we'd be

run over by a car. But after she picked up speed, I was afraid that a car would be run over by us. And one was! We banged into a pickup truck driven by an angry kiwi and went flying into the air.

"This plan is too daring!" I yelled in midair.

"This isn't actually part of the plan," she answered, still in midair.

We landed in a heap in front of the Fancy Froo Froo Hotel and Disco.

"But here we are anyway," she said.

We went inside.

"Excuse me," she asked the moose behind the front desk. "Could you call up to Countess Zuzu Poodle-oo's room and ask her butler to come down here?"

The moose took a deep breath and yelled, "DJ FUNKYFOOT, YOU ARE WANTED IN THE FRONT LOBBY BY A COUPLE OF DODOS!"

Several minutes later, the elevator

doors opened, and a very serious-looking Chihuahua came out.

"How may I be of service?" the Chihuahua asked stiffly.

"Smell this," Didi said, handing him the empty jar.

He took a big sniff.

"Can you tell us what was in it?" Didi asked.

"Yes, miss."

"And can you tell us the answer by rapping?" I asked.

"I regret to say that I cannot, sir."

"Why not?"

"Because I cannot think of anything that rhymes with Cousin Yuk Yuk's Pickled Rhubarb Relish."

PART 2
Dodos Don't Fly

Chapter 4

"Where are we going now?" I yelled as Didi Dodo skated us out of town.

"To Cousin Yuk Yuk's Pickled Rhubarb Relish Farm!" she shouted back. "It's down in Dangerously Steep Valley."

"How far down?"

"All the way down!"

All the way down was a long way down!

And we kept picking up speed as we went!

"This is TOO daring!" I yelled.

And then the pavement ended and the road became a dirt road.

Now we were picking up speed and going *whumpita-whumpita-whumpita!*

"Are you kidding me with this *whumpita-whumpita-whumpita*! Please, slow down!" I yelled.

"I don't know how to slow down!"

I remembered how she had landed in my snickerdoodle dough.

"I am guessing you don't know how to stop, either!" I shouted.

"Nope!" she shouted back.

"Do you know how to dodge that cow that is in the middle of the road?"

"No!" she shouted back. "But my daring plan is for you to jump and for me to duck!"

I jumped. She ducked. The cow took a photo of us with her phone.

"You crazy birds are in big trouble now!" the cow said. "I'm going to post this on FaceMoo and my 51,008 friends are all going to write rude comments about you!"

"We've got bigger problems than that!" I shouted back. "The bridge is out up ahead and we can't stop!"

"Can't you just fly away?" yelled the cow.

"No, dodos can't fly!" I yelled back.

"Wow, you're in big trouble!" yelled the cow. "If you die, I'll tell my 51,008 friends not to be too rude about it."

"THAAAAAAAAAANNNNNKSSS!" I yelled as we zoomed over the edge of the road and plunged down down down down down down and down into Dangerously Steep Valley.

Chapter 5

I told you it was too daring!" I shouted. "Now, we're falling to our DOOM!"

"No," said Didi Dodo. "We are falling to our relish!"

"Our relish? What are you telling me about—"

"Just look down," she said.

"I don't want to. I'm afraid of heights."

"Well," she said. "We're not as high up as we used to be . . ."

I looked down. She was right. We weren't that high up anymore.

"We're about to hit the ground!" I shouted.

"No," said Didi Dodo. "We're about to hit the relish."

"Why do you keep talking about relish?"

"Because we are about to land in a giant vat of it," said Didi Dodo. "You may

want to hold your nose. And close your eyes."

Well, that was the first sensible thing she had said all day.

Splash!

Chapter 6

WHUT ARE YOO BURDS DOON IN MAH RELISH?" bellowed a very angry yak wearing a three-piece suit.

"Trying to swim!" I cried, trying to swim.

The yak grabbed us both by the beaks, yanked us out of the vat, and tossed us on the ground.

"YOO BURDS JUS ROONED YUK YUK'S RELISH!"

"Are you Cousin Yuk Yuk?" I gasped.

"OF COORSE I AM CUZIN YUK YUK! NOW SHUT UP AN TELL ME WHAT YOO DUM BURDS ARE DOIN!"

"Uh . . . I . . ." I sputtered. I did not know how to answer his question without making him even more angry.

I looked at Didi. Why wasn't she saying anything? Aren't spies supposed to be able to talk themselves out of trouble?

But after talking fast all morning, she now had her beak shut tight!

It was up to me.

I held up the empty jar.

"We'd like to buy some relish."

"YOO ROONED A WHOLE VAT OF REL-ISH JUSTA BUY A TINY JARFUL?!"

"Uh . . . yes?" I whimpered.

He roared, "I'M GUNNA STUFF YOO IN THAT JAR, BURD!"

"Please do not do that! I will not fit in the jar!"

"YOO WILL AFFER I STOOMP YOO!"

Cousin Yuk Yuk lowered his head and charged at us!

Didi waved her wings around like she was trying to tell me something.

"Are you saying that you have a daring

plan to escape and that I should jump on your back and you'll skate between the yak's legs at the last second and then we'll zoom around the vat, race through the barn, rush past the other angry yaks that are headed this way, jump over the manure pile, bounce over the fence, and escape?" I asked.

She nodded.

"OK," I said. "While it is daring, it actually seems less daring than staying here and getting stoomped. Let's do it!"

And we did. JUST BARELY!

Interlude

W ell, your daring plan half worked," I said. "We got away from the herd of angry yaks, but . . . we didn't get any rhubarb relish and now I can't make the—"

Didi waved at me to be quiet.

Then she waved at me to hold out the jar and remove the lid.

Then she spat out a whole beakful of pickled rhubarb relish into the jar.

"Gross!" I said.

"You're telling me!" said Didi. "I hate rhubarb! But now you have your secret ingredient! You can make your fudge sauce, put it on your cookies, and win the Queen's Royal Cookie Contest!"

"You're right!" I shouted.

Then I thought about it.

"You're wrong," I whimpered.

"What now?" she asked.

"Well," I said. "First, I don't have any cookies because we didn't finish baking them!"

"No problem . . ."

"Second, I have my secret ingredient for the fudge sauce, but now I don't have any other ingredients!"

"No problem . . ."

"Third, the contest starts in an hour and we're miles and miles away from the mall!"

"No problem . . ."

"Fourth, we're at the bottom of a road that is too steep to skate up!"

"No problem . . ."

"And fifth, the herd of angry yaks has knocked down the fence and is charging at us again!"

"No problem!"

"What are you telling me 'no problem' for?" I yelled. "Yes, these are problems!"

"And here comes the solution," said Didi Dodo. She pointed at a food truck zooming straight at us!

She waved the truck down with her wing.

The brakes screeched!

The truck spun!

Didi grabbed me and jumped!

We sailed through the open window and landed in a comfy seat.

"Welcome to Penguini's Food Truck, my friends," said the driver, a penguin, stomping on the gas and driving way too fast up the curvy road out of Dangerously

Steep Valley. "Would you care for an appetizer?"

"Thanks, Penguini," said Didi Dodo, eating a stuffed mushroom. "Do you mind if Koko Dodo uses your kitchen while you drive us to the Royal Cookie Contest at the mall?"

"It would be an honor," said Penguini. "But he may want to wait until after we've jumped over the broken bridge. It may be a little bumpy."

Koko Dodo's Super SECRET Fudge Sauce

Approved by Her Royal Majesty, the Queen

This recipe makes enough fudge sauce to spread on three cookies or one taco.

YOU WILL NEED:

- Two bowls
- Whisk (or a fork will do if you are patient)
- Measuring spoons
- Strainer (again, a fork will do if you are REALLY patient)
- Three cookies (or one taco)

INGREDIENTS:

- Cousin Yuk Yuk's Pickle Relish. If you can't find Cousin Yuk Yuk's brand, try another brand, such as Mama Smedlap's Chow-Chow or Dusty's Sweet Gherkin Goop.

- Milk

- Instant Chocolate Pudding Mix

INSTRUCTIONS:

1) Use a measuring spoon to put three teaspoons of relish in a bowl.

2) Next, use the same spoon to add five teaspoons of milk.

3) Use the whisk, or fork, to stir and smoosh the relish and the milk. The more you smoosh the better the flavor! Continue until the milk has turned a gross yellow-green color and is full of stinky lumps.

4) Hold the strainer over the empty bowl. Now pour the lumpy pickle-milk through the strainer. You now have a bowl of delicious pickle milk without the lumps! (If you don't have a strainer, use a fork to pick out the lumps.)

5) Add two teaspoons of pudding mix to the bowl and use the whisk to stir it all together. When the mixture is nice and thick, set it aside for 3 minutes. (Use the time to throw the pickle lumps into the trash before someone comes along and complains about the stink.)

6) Finally, spread the fudge sauce on a cookie and enjoy!

PART 3

Food Court Royale

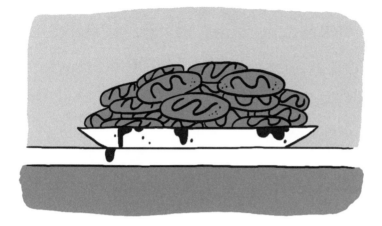

Chapter 7

A re you kidding me? It was a lot bumpy!

But I baked some oatmeal raisin cookies and made the fudge sauce in the tiny kitchen in the back of Penguini's food truck. It is not so easy drizzling fudge sauce on cookies when you are in the back of a truck driven by a fast and furious penguin, let me tell you!

"Three minutes to spare," said Penguini as he screeched the food truck into the mall parking lot.

"Three minutes?!" I yelled. "What are you telling me with the three minutes?"

"The contest starts at noon, right?"

"Right!"

"Well, right now the clock says 11:57! So, I got you here with three minutes to spare!"

"But the contest is INSIDE and we are OUTSIDE! What are we going to do, Didi?"

"Don't worry," she said. "I have a daring plan! Koko, grab the cookies and jump on my back. Penguini, put the truck in reverse. Full speed!"

"This plan is TOO daring!" I told Didi.

"This plan is TOO daring!" Penguini told Didi.

"Thank you," said Didi. "Now hit the brakes, Penguini."

Penguini hit the brakes. The back doors flew open and we flew out!

I know I said dodos can't fly, but for a minute it felt like we could!

Then we landed with a *whump* and I lost several of the cookies! But we kept rolling at some kind of crazy speed. The number is so high I cannot even tell you.

"Hey! Teenage Rooster! Open the mall door!" Didi shouted, and a Teenage Rooster opened the mall door just in time.

"Watch out for the Mall Cop, dudes. He's mean," Teenage Rooster shouted, grabbing a cookie as we went by.

We whooshed inside, spilling more cookies along the way and bumping into many, many chickens. (This mall is very popular with chickens.)

"Where's the cookie contest, Cute Baby Chicks?" yelled Didi Dodo.

"It's in the Royal Food Court," chirped the Cute Baby Chicks, grabbing cookies as

we went by. "We'd come with you, but we can't go there, because the mean Mall Cop kicked us out for pooping on the chairs. But we can't help it, we're just—"

We didn't hear any more, because Didi Dodo just kept on skating faster and faster.

"Which way to the Royal Food Court, Sweet Old Hen?" Didi shouted, and a Sweet Old Hen pointed to a down escalator.

"Better not let the Mall Cop see you on

those roller skates, dearie," said the Sweet
Old Hen, grabbing a cookie as we went by.

Didi steered straight for the escalator!

"No! You're going too fast! Please don't
do it!" I begged. "It's just TOO daring!"

She did it.

*WHUP . . . WHAP . . . WHUG . . .
WHAMMM!* We bounced down the escalator steps!

KRASMASH! We landed on Ye Olde Pretzel Cart!

SHPLASHPILL! Hot butter went everywhere! So did the rest of my cookies! I let go of Didi and just barely grabbed the last one.

WHOOSHOOOOOOOOP! I fell off Didi's back, landed in the hot butter, and slid into the Royal Food Court!

Chapter 8

I slid past Ye Olde Frozen Yogurt Palace.

I slid past Ye Olde Jester Jim's Juice Hut.

I slid past Ye Olde Tacos on a Stick.

I slid past Ye Olde Cookie Castle. (Not as good as mine, trust me.)

I slid past Ye Olde Deep Fried Dungeon.

And, at last, I slid to a stop at the feet of

a duck wearing a crown. The Queen of the Royal Food Court!

I staggered to my feet and held the final cookie in the air!

"Here!" I shouted. "Here is my cookie, Your Majesty!"

I handed her the cookie.

She ate it.

She smiled a queenly smile.

"Thank you, flightless bird. That was the best cookie I have ever eaten."

"What are you telling me? Did I win the contest?"

"No," she said. "You MISSED the contest. It ended thirteen seconds before you handed me that cookie."

"But . . ."

"SILENCE! The Queen has spoken!"

Chapter 9

started to cry.

All the hard work! All the daring plans! All the relish! All for nothing!

"I'm sorry, Koko," said Didi Dodo. "I tried, but . . . I guess you needed a real spy. Not a future spy."

Then Didi Dodo started to cry, too.

We sat there in a puddle of lukewarm butter and wept.

My phone rang.

"Hello, this is Koko Dodo. What are you telling me?" I sniffled.

"Koko Dodo! It is me, Inspector Flytrap! I am checking to see if you caught the thief who stole your fudge sauce!"

"I don't care anymore," I sobbed.

"You don't care?" asked Flytrap. "What about justice?"

"I don't care about justice!"

"Justice is a very big deal!" said Flytrap. "I'd say more, but I have to go stop Nina from eating my grandmother. Good-bye!"

"Inspector Flytrap is right," I told Didi Dodo. "Justice is a big deal. What about your daring plan to figure out who the thief was?"

"Well," said Didi Dodo. "My daring plan was to catch whoever DID win the contest, because they must have used your fudge sauce."

"Excuse me," I said to the Queen. "Who won the contest?"

"No one," said the Queen.

"No one?"

"No," she said. "No one entered."

"Why not?" I asked.

"Why should they enter when you win every year?"

I had not thought about that. I looked around and saw that no one was paying any attention to the contest. No one cared who won, because I always won. Well, except for this time.

"Since no one won," said the Queen, "I get to keep the trophy and—more important—the large cash prize! Buh-bye."

The Queen hiked up her dress and waddled out of the food court, tossing the trophy in a trash can on her way.

"That daring plan didn't work, either!" cried Didi. "You didn't win, and I didn't catch the thief. The whole thing is a big poo-poo!"

"What are you telling me about the poo-poo?" I asked.

"What I am telling you," said Didi Dodo, "is that the whole thing makes no sense! If someone didn't steal the fudge sauce to win the contest, then WHY did someone steal the fudge sauce?"

"I guess it was someone who really, really, really, really likes fudge sauce made with pickled rhubarb relish," I said.

Didi looked up.

She wiped away the tears.

She waved one wing in the air.

She held her beak high.

Her eyes sparkled and so did the cold and clammy butter sauce stuck in her feathers.

"I know who stole the fudge sauce AND I have a daring plan to catch them!" she shouted.

Where Dodos Dare

Chapter 10

STOP THAT DUCK!" Didi yelled.

"The Queen?" I gasped.

"Yes!" exclaimed Didi. "She's the one who loves the secret fudge sauce more than anybody! She loves it so much that she gave you the prize every year! But this year she got greedy. She wanted the secret sauce AND the cash prize!"

"Well, that was mean!" I said.

"Yes, it was! But we'll bring her to justice!" said Didi. Then she shouted again, "STOP THAT DUCK!"

But none of the mall customers tried to stop the Queen. In fact, they just ignored us and kept on shopping.

"We've got to do it ourselves!" said Didi. "Hop on."

I jumped on her back.

"Are you leaving already?" gasped Penguini, sliding into the food court on the spilled butter. "I finally got the food truck parked!"

"We're not leaving, we're chasing a duck," said Didi Dodo. "Hop on!"

"OK," said Penguini, and he hopped on my back.

"Can we come, too?" asked the Cute

Baby Chicks. "We snuck down here to see the cookie contest—and to poop on the chairs—and now we need to get out of here fast, before the Mall Cop catches us."

"Yes, but hurry," said Didi. "The Queen is getting away!"

The chicks hopped on Penguini's back.

Didi started skating . . . straight into Papa Pelican's Ye Olde Hot Dog Stand.

"Ye hast knocketh down my frankfurters!" yelled Papa Pelican.

"Sorry!" she said. "It's hard to steer with a dodo, a penguin, and Cute Baby Chicks on my back."

"No problem," said the Cute Baby Chicks, chomping down on hot dogs. "We were hungry anyway."

"But the Queen is getting away!" I yelled.

"Not if my daring plan works!" yelled Didi, wing raised, beak high, eyes sparkling.

She pushed off from the hot dog stand and built up speed, and soon we were zooming through the crowd.

"Ye chicks forgoteth to pay for thy hot dogs!" I heard Papa Pelican shouting behind us. "I'm calling the Mall Cop!"

"Uh-oh," said the chicks.

Chapter 11

There goes the Queen!" I shouted.

The Queen was running into a store called Barney's Breakables.

Didi made a hard turn, and we just barely held on to each other.

We screeched into Barney's Breakables.

CRACK! CRUNCH! SHATTER!

Many things were broken.

Many, many things.

The Queen ran out. We skated out. Barney wept.

"Boo hoo hoo," cried Barney. "I'm calling the Mall Cop on you!"

"Uh-oh," said the Cute Baby Chicks.

"There she is!" I shouted.

The Queen was running into a store called Leroy's Extremely Clean Chairs!

I would rather not say what happened next, but it was gross.

"My chairs!" yelled Leroy. "Look at what those chicks did to my chairs!"

The Queen ran out.

We skated out.

Leroy screamed, "I'm calling the Mall Cop!"

"Uh-oh," said the Cute Baby Chicks.

The Queen ran into a glass elevator.

We tried to follow her, but the doors closed just before we got there.

The Queen gave us a royal wave as the elevator carried her up to the next floor.

"We've got to get up there!" said Didi Dodo, swerving. "And we don't have time to wait for the elevator. I'm going to use that Cheese Booth as a ramp and try to jump up to the next level."

"Can you make it?" I asked. It looked way too high!

"No," she said. "But you can . . . with a Triple Koko."

"What are you telling me with the Triple Koko?!" I shouted. "I've never done a Triple Koko on roller skates!"

"It's pretty much the same thing," said Didi Dodo. "Plus, the wheels are coated in butter, so it's just like sliding on ice."

"OK, I'll try," I said. "Just stop so I can put on the skates."

"I don't know how to stop," said Didi Dodo, "but I do have a daring plan."

"Uh-oh," said the chicks.

Didi skated on one foot and took off the skate from her other foot.

"Put this on and get ready to switch," she told me.

I laced up the skate while she swerved around chicken shoppers and knocked over a display rack of priceless crystal donkeys.

Then I started skating on one foot, while Didi hopped along beside us, took off her other skate, and put it on my foot. Then she climbed up on top of me, Penguini, the Cute Baby Chicks, and the Sweet Old Hen, who had somehow hitched a ride with us.

"Be careful, dearie," said the Sweet Old Hen.

"That's not part of my daring plan," said Didi Dodo. "But this is . . . Now, Koko!"

We hit the slanted side of the Cheese Booth and whooshed into the air.

I twisted and twirled and felt Penguini grabbing on to my leg.

"That's one Koko!" yelled Didi.

I twirled and twisted and saw Didi trying to hold the Cute Baby Chicks under her wing.

"That's two Kokos!" yelled Didi. "We've almost made it!"

I twisted, but Penguini was losing his grip. If I twirled, he would fall, and so would Didi and the chicks!

So instead of twirling, I twisted again. I had invented a new trick! I could call it the Quadruple Koko, or maybe the Dodo Double Double, or maybe the . . .

But before I could decide, we were zooming up and over the railing!

We had made it to the second floor! But because I had missed a twirl, I didn't land on the skates.

I landed on Penguini.

Penguini landed on the Sweet Old Hen.

The Sweet Old Hen landed on the chicks.

The chicks landed on Didi Dodo.

And Didi Dodo landed on the Queen!

"Quack!" said the Queen.

"We did it!" Didi Dodo and I yelled.

"Please get off me, dearie," the Sweet Old Hen said to Penguini.

"I am so sorry, madam," Penguini replied.

"YOU BURDS ARE IN BIG TRUBBLE!" shouted the Mall Cop.

"Uh-oh," the Cute Baby Chicks chirped.

Chapter 12

The Mall Cop looked a lot like Cousin Yuk Yuk!

"Are you Cousin Yuk Yuk?" I asked.

"OF COORSE I AM CUZIN YUK YUK!"

"What are you doing here?"

"Well, the relish business has been slow, so I took this job to make extra money," he said. "NOW SHUD UP SO I CAN YELL AT YOO!"

All of us, except for Didi Dodo, trembled in fear.

"YOO," he yelled at the Queen, "ARE FIRED!"

He grabbed the crown off her head and balled it up. It was just cardboard.

The Queen cried.

"YOO," he yelled at Penguini, "ARE PARKED IN A LOADIN ZONE! THEY ARE TOWIN YOOR FOOD TRUCK AWAY!"

Penguini cried.

"YOO," he yelled at the Cute Baby

Chicks and the Sweet Old Hen, "ARE BANNED FROM THA FOOD COURT FOR LIFE!"

The Sweet Old Hen cried. The Cute Baby Chicks said "Uh-oh," and then they cried.

"BUT YOO TWO," he yelled at Didi and me, "ARE IN THA MOST TRUBBLE OF ALL! DO YOO KNOW HOW MUTCH DAMAGE YOO HAVE DUN TO THA MALL?"

"Uh . . . no?" I said.

"FIVE HUNDERD AN THREE DOLLURS AN THURTY-SEVEN CENTS' WORTH! NOW PAY UP OR GO TO JAIL!"

The Mall Cop got out a tiny notebook and started writing in it.

I cried.

Didi Dodo did not cry.

"I've got a daring plan," she whispered, quietly switching the skates back to her own feet.

Then she yelled, "Jump on, everybody! Let's make a break for it!"

"Wait!" said the Queen. "I've got a better plan. Koko Dodo, you deserved to win the cookie contest. Here is the prize money . . . five hundred dollars!"

"What are you telling me, Your Royal Highness?" I asked.

"I got too greedy and now everybody is in trouble. It was my fault, so let me fix it," she said. And even though she didn't have her crown, she still seemed a lot like a royal duck. "You can take the prize money and use it to pay for the damages."

She handed me the money bag full of five hundred dollars.

I handed the bag to the Mall Cop.

"WHUT ABOUT THE UTHER THREE DOLLURS AN THURTY-SEVEN CENTS?" he yelled.

I checked my pockets. I didn't have any money. (Or any pockets!)

"WELL?" roared the Mall Cop. "DO YOO HAVE THE MONEY OR DO I GIT TO STOOMP YOO?"

I looked at Didi. She didn't have any money, but from the way she was waving her wing and holding her beak and shining her eyes, I knew that she had a daring plan.

She did.

Epilogue

After we escaped the Mall Cop, grabbed the trophy from the trash can, and rescued Penguini's food truck, we all went back to my cookie shop.

"Just a minute," I said, turning on the oven, "and we'll have hot cookies!"

"I hope they are old-fashioned sugar cookies," said the Sweet Old Hen.

"Yes," I said. "They are!"

"Will they have rainbow sprinkles?" asked the chicks.

"Yes," I said. "They will!"

"Mmm-mmm," said the chicks.

While the cookies baked, I put the new trophy with the other trophies.

"My last trophy," I said. "Next year, I will let someone else win."

"Also, you'll be arrested if you ever go to the mall again," said the Queen. "And . . . so will I."

The Queen started to cry.

"Since you lost your job," I said, "maybe you'd like to be my assistant baker."

The Queen stopped crying.

"Will you teach me how to make the secret fudge sauce?" she asked.

"Maybe," I said. "But first you must learn how to take hot sugar cookies with sprinkles out of the oven."

I handed her the oven mitts and she went to work.

"It's a good thing you hired an assistant," said Didi Dodo. "Because you are going to be very busy!"

"What are you telling me with the busy?" I asked.

She handed me a card.

It said:

Dodo & Dodo
Future Spies
(And licensed babysitter and award-winning cookie baker)

"This is a daring plan," I said. "And I like it!"

Then we all had cookies.

Dodo and Dodo are back in book #2:

Robo-Dodo Rumble!

Here's a sneak peek.

Opening

My phone rang.

"Hello, this is Koko Dodo's Cookie Shop. Koko Dodo speaking! What are you telling me?" I said.

"How-dee, neigh-bor," said a robot voice. "Would you like to—"

"Wait just a minute!" I interrupted. "Is this one of those robocalls?"

"What is a ro-bo-call?" asked the robot voice.

"You know! One of those awful calls where you answer the phone and all you hear is a recording and the recording wants to sell you something."

"This is not a re-cor-ding," said the robot voice.

"But you sound a lot like a robot!"

"I AM a ro-bot."

"Oh, well that explains it," I said. "Sorry if I was rude. I just hate those calls that try to sell you something. So . . . What do you want?"

"I want to sell you some-thing," said the robot. "I am sell-ing coo-kies."

"Cookies? What are you telling me about cookies? I am Koko Dodo! I bake my own cookies in my own cookie shop! Of course I do not want to buy any cookies!"

"O-kay, I will find some-one else to buy my coo-kies. Good-bye, neigh-bor."

The robot hung up.

I went back to baking my own cookies, but I kept wondering: Why did the robot keep calling me "neighbor"?

PART 1

The Price Is Wrong

Chapter 1

It was a slow morning at the cookie shop.

I had been baking for hours with my helper, the Queen. We had made many, many cookies.

But we did not have many, many customers.

In fact, we did not have ANY customers.

"Where are all the customers, Your Majesty?" I asked.

"I don't know, Koko," said the Queen. "Even the three baby chicks haven't been here!"

"Well, at least we won't have to clean the baby chick poop off the chairs today," I said. "But what are we going to do with all these uneaten cookies? I'll go out of business this way!"

"Wait," said the Queen. "Someone's coming!"

I opened the door.

"Hello and welcome to—"

"Look out!" said Didi Dodo, who was the someone who was coming. And boy was she coming fast!

She zoomed through the door on her

roller skates and crashed into the counter. Unsold cookies went everywhere!

The Queen was hit on the head by a double-chocolate chunk cookie! She would have been knocked out if her cardboard crown hadn't protected her.

"Sorry about the cookies," said Didi Dodo.

SLAM

"Don't be worrying about it!" I said. "No one was buying them. You're the first customer we've had all day!"

"Sorry, Koko," said Didi. "I didn't come to buy cookies. I came because . . ."

Didi Dodo sprang to her feet—actually, to her wheels—and waved one wing in the air.

She held her beak high.

Her eyes sparkled.

"I, Didi Dodo, Future Spy, have a daring plan!" she shouted.

"I need customers, not a daring plan!"

"But my daring plan is to get your customers back!"

"Get them back from where?" I asked.

"From there!" she said and pointed her wing out the window and across the street.

Chapter 2

I looked out the window and saw a giant dodo across the street!

"There's a giant dodo across the street!" I yelled.

"No," said Didi Dodo. "There's a giant Robo-Dodo across the street!"

"What are you telling me about a Robo-Dodo?" I yelled. "What is a Robo-Dodo?"

"A Robo-Dodo is a very large robot that is shaped like a dodo and sells cheap cookies."

"CHEAP COOKIES?!" I screamed. "No wonder I lost all my customers! How cheap are they?"

Just then, an elephant wearing a top hat ran past the store. His mouth was full, and cookie crumbs were falling out.

Didi opened the door and said, "Excuse me, how much did those cookies cost?"

"A penny," said the elephant wearing a top hat.

"COOKIES FOR A PENNY EACH?!" I yelled.

"No," said the elephant. "All the cookies you can eat for one penny!"

"ALL THE COOKIES YOU CAN EAT FOR ONE PENNY?! I AM RUINED! I WILL HAVE TO CLOSE MY SHOP!"

"Just a second!" demanded the Queen. "How do the cookies taste?"

"Oh, they're terrible," said the elephant. "Like chewing moldy bricks."

"What are you telling me with the moldy bricks?" I asked. "Wouldn't you rather have one of my delicious, fresh peanut butter yumyums?"

"How much?" asked the elephant.

"Only $1.59," I said.

"What a rip-off!" yelled the elephant. "I can eat robot cookies for 159 days for that much! Now, if you'll excuse me, I'm going back for more!"

The elephant stampeded across the street.

"Didi Dodo," I said.

"Yes, Koko Dodo?" she said, her eye already sparkling.

"I need a daring plan."

"I have one!" she shouted.

ABOUT THE AUTHOR AND ILLUSTRATOR

TOM ANGLEBERGER is the *New York Times* bestselling author of the Origami Yoda series, as well as many other books for kids. He created Koko Dodo with his wife, Cece Bell, for the Inspector Flytrap series. When that series ended, he still wanted to send Koko on some bigger adventures . . . whether Koko wanted to go or not! Visit Tom at origamiyoda.com.

JARED CHAPMAN is the author-illustrator of the best-selling *Vegetables in Underwear*, as well as *Fruits in Suits* and *Pirate, Viking & Scientist*. He lives in Texas. Find out more about Jared at jaredchapman.com.